THE NEW
FRANKENSTEIN

BY

E. E. KELLETT

British Library Cataloguing-in-Publication Data
A catalogue record for this book is available from
the British Library

Contents

E. E. KELLETT

Ernest Edward Kellett was born in 1864. Little is known about his life, other than that, in his day, he was a respected literary critic. Amongst his most well-known works are *The Whirligig of Taste* (1929), *Fashion in Literature: A Study of Changing Taste* (1931), *A Short History of Religions* (1933), As *I Remember* (1936) and *Aspects of History* (1938). He also wrote a fairly popular collection of spooky stories, entitled *A Corner in Sleep and Other Impossibilities* (1900).

The New Frankenstein

By E.E. KELLETT

'YES,' SAID ARTHUR, 'I feel very much inclined to try it.'
The speaker, Arthur Moore, was a man whom I was proud to call my friend. Early in life he had distinguished himself by many wonderful inventions. When a boy he had adorned his bedroom with all sorts of curious mechanical contrivances: pulleys for lifting unheard-of weights, rat-traps which, by cunning devices, provided the captured animal with a silent and painless euthanasia; locomotives, which when once wound up, would run for a day, and numberless other treasures, which, if hardly useful or even ornamental, had yet the effect of inspiring the housemaid who made the bed, with a mortal terror of everything in the room. As he grew older he lost none of his skill. At the age of fifteen he had successfully emulated most of the feats of Vaucanson; his mechanical ducks gobbled and digested their food so naturally that even the famous scientist, the Rev. Henry Forest, was for a moment taken in. He had been to Oxford, but after a year of University life, he had wearied of the dull routine, and had begged his father to let him start life on his own account. His father need have had no fear for the result. Within a year the young Moore's automatic chess-player, that had played a draw with Morphy himself, had attracted the awestruck attention of the civilised world by the simplicity and daring of its mechanism. The chess-player was followed in two years by a whist-player, still more simply and boldly conceived; and after that time scarcely a year had passed without being signalised by the appearance of new wonders from Moore's fertile brain and dextrous hand. His last achievement had been a phonograph so perfectly constructed that people began to think that even Edison must soon begin to look to his laurels, or he would be eclipsed by the rising fame of this young man of thirty.

I had known him since he was a boy; and had kept my acquaintance with him in spite of the ever-widening difference between our paths and our beliefs. I had chosen the medical profession, and after a year or two of early struggles, was at last beginning to see my way to an assured reputation, and a fair competency. In fact, I was already a fashionable doctor, pretty well known by the public, and I hope pretty well esteemed by the profession.

It was just after the new phonograph had appeared that I had with Arthur the memorable and unfortunate conversation which I shall regret to the very end of my life.

'Well,' I said, 'a new and great success again. You will be one of the greatest benefactors of the century in a few years.'

'Yes,' he answered, for he had no false modesty. 'I believe the phonograph is about as perfect as I can make it. Suppose we listen to it now.'

He produced the instrument, and I had the pleasure of listening to a speech of Mr Gladstone's, with the familiar tones and inflections of the great orator reproduced to the life. I could have believed I saw the Grand Old Man before me, as I had seen him so often.

'Wonderful,' said. 'It is indeed perfect. What a strange, almost uncanny thing it is! We shall soon have to be very careful what we say; for a bird of the air shall carry the voice, and that which hath wings shall tell the matter. Fancy what a preventive of crime a phonograph fastened on every lamp-post would be! It would be a kind of Magic Flute, forcing people to tell the truth whether they would or no. Jones might say, "I said this," but the phonograph would say, "You said that." Mere human fallible creatures will soon be banished from the witness-box; judges and juries will content themselves with taking the evidence of unerring, unlying phonographs!'

'Heaven save us!' Moore replied; 'all of us say many things that will hardly bear repeating; and if they are all to be recorded, how dreadful it would be.'

'Yes; you see you are after all but a doubtful benefactor of the human race; it is not everybody who, like Job, can wish that his words were now written.'

'Nor Job himself at all times,' he answered: 'perhaps he would hardly have wished to have recorded the words he used when he cursed his day.'

'In fact,' I said, 'what is a phonograph after all but a tattling old woman, repeating whatever it hears without discrimination or tact?'

'Exactly,' he said; 'but with this difference, that the phonograph repeats what it hears without alteration or addition, whereas the old woman repeats it just as it suits her.'

At this moment the fatal idea struck me, which now I would give worlds to have forgotten or suppressed before it came to the birth. Alas, we know not the results of our least words.

'Why,' I said, 'don't you try to make a kind of complement of a phonograph?'

'What do you mean?'

'Why, this. Your phonograph only repeats what it hears. Why not make an instrument which should, not *repeat* words, but speak out the suitable answer to them? If, for instance, I were to say to it "Good morning, have you used Pears' Soap?" then why should it not answer, "No, I use Cleaver's," instead of merely reiterating my words? At present, your machine is nothing but an echo; glorious, I grant; a triumph of civilisation; but what an achievement it would be to contrive a sort of anti-phonograph, that should give the appropriate *answer* to each question I like to put!'

'Why, a thing that could do that would be nothing less than man.'

'Well,' I said, 'what *is* man but a bundle of sensations – a machine that answers pretty accurately to the questions daily put to it?' For I was, or pretended to be, a full-blown materialist.

'It may be so,' he answered; 'yet it seems to me that he is a very complex machine for all that. He has taken thousands of years to evolve, if what Darwin says is true; you ask me to make him in at most a year or two.'

'Listen to me,' I said, half in irony, half in earnest. 'When you made your whist-player, what did you do but calculate on a certain number of actions, all theoretically possible, and arrange that the machine should give the proper answer to them?'

'True.'

'And with your chess-player, was it not the same?'

'Exactly.'

'Well, then, the principle is granted. Allow that a certain number of phrases may be used; let your machine give the proper answer to them. Don't you see the analogy? Had it been impossible for the machine to speak, I should have been satisfied with your disclaimers; but your phonograph has settled that.'

'The number of sentences is infinite.'

'A detail, my friend. Are there not, practically, infinite varieties of hands at whist? Yet your automaton never made a mistake. Are there not infinite varieties of number? Yet did that puzzle Babbage's calculating machine?'

'You may be right, Phillips,' he said, smiling at my earnestness. 'I will think of it.'

I took my leave, little dreaming that I had set in motion a mighty force which would bring misery to more than a few. Indeed, I completely forgot the whole conversation. It was not till several months later that, happening to meet Moore in the street, I was suddenly startled by hearing the words I have already mentioned.

'Yes, I feel very much inclined to try it.'

'To try what?' I said, completely bewildered.

'Why, the thing we were talking of some months ago.'

'Do you mean to say you have been thinking of it?' I said. 'Why, I had utterly forgotten it.'

'Thought of it, yes; and worked at it, which is more. I see my way to something very like it, at any rate.'

'Go on,' I said, becoming interested. 'This is the most wonderful thing you have done yet, if –'

'Listen,' he interrupted. 'Words are nothing but air-vibrations, are they?'

'Nothing,' I answered.

'Well, then, it follows that words, if put in the proper positions, can generate motion.'

'I follow you; a molecular windmill.'

'Well,' he said, 'this is the idea of my machine. Words are spoken into the ear of my automaton. Passing through the ear they enter a machine you would call an anti-phonograph, and set in motion various processes which in a very short time produce the words constituting the proper answer.'

'Wonderful,' I said, 'if true.'

'Come and see then,' he rejoined, 'if you will be so sceptical.'

I followed him to his workshop, and saw a small instrument, in its main external details exactly like a phonograph.

'This,' said Moore, 'is the centre of my automaton. Try it yourself. Ask it a question – anything you like.'

Wondering, I did as he suggested. There was a tube on each side of the instrument, communicating with its centre, which I supposed would form the 'ear' of the automaton when finished. I was at a loss how to begin the conversation; but, being an Englishman, called the weather to my aid.

'A very cold day,' I remarked.

A sweet and beautifully modulated feminine voice answered:

'Yes; but hardly so cold as yesterday.'

I started, as though I had seen a ghost. Had I not been a doctor, old as I was, I should have precipitately fled. But it takes a good deal to shake the nerves of a physician. In an instant I recovered myself.

'Moore,' I said, 'you can't play with me. You are ventriloquising.'

He was very indignant.

'What do you think of me?' he said. '*I* to go playing the tricks of a strolling mountebank! What the devil!'

'I beg your pardon,' I replied. 'But you must acknowledge that on the Baconian principle one must acknowledge no new cause until the possibility of all known causes has been eliminated. Now ventriloquism, vulgar or not, is a known agent; your principle, whatever it be, is perfectly new. So that you can hardly blame me.'

'I swear,' he said, 'that I have had nothing to do with the thing since you came into the room, and that while you were speaking to it I never opened my mouth.'

'Never mind, I believe you fully.'

'You shall take it with you,' he replied, 'and try it in your own rooms, if you doubt me.'

'Not a bit,' I replied. 'Still, I will take it, in order that the outside world may be convinced.'

'You shall; but try it again here, and see for yourself again. I will not open my mouth.'

I tried again, a certain uncanny feeling still possessing me. Oh, for the inventive powers of a Frenchman, in order to begin the conversation naturally!

'That was a fine speech of Mr Gladstone's yesterday evening.'

'Yes,' the delicate feminine voice again replied; 'I didn't read it all, but the beginning and the end were very good, weren't they?'

Again the same eerie feeling came over me, followed as before by the conviction that some trickery must be at the bottom of this most unparalleled experience. I looked at Moore. He was sitting in his armchair by the fire, a smile playing on his face; but his lips were set fast.

I tried yet a third time, determined to watch Moore's face during the whole operation.

'Mr Gladstone must be old now,' I said rather inanely.

'Seventy-nine last birthday,' replied the voice, *precisely at the same moment as Moore was saying*,

'By Jove, eighty-five if he is a day!'

I was convinced by that. No human being ever spoke two sentences precisely at the same instant. Either there was somebody else in the room, or Moore had succeeded, marvellously succeeded. He had made an instrument that could not only imitate the tones of the human voice, but could keep up a conversation as constantly, if not as wittily, as Miss Notable and Mr Neverout in Swift's *Polite Conversation*.

'Satisfied, old fellow?' said Moore, rising from his chair and coming toward me.

'Are you sure there is no one else in the room?' I said.

'Search,' he replied, a little contemptuously, as though half amused, half wearied by my recurring scepticism.

But I was too well acquainted with Moore's earnest and honourable nature to doubt him any more.

'My dear fellow,' I said, 'I know you are incapable of deception. I take your word. On anything else I would take your nod or shake of the head. But this is extraordinary, very extraordinary. I never heard anything like it.'

'No more did I,' he replied with pardonable vanity, 'until a week or so ago. I had tried all kinds of devices to make the thing answer sensibly; she would answer, of course, long ago, but I wanted her to behave like a lady, not like a lunatic.'

'So you mean your automaton to be a lady, do you?'

'Yes,' he replied, drawing closer. 'And I want her to be a lady that would deceive the Queen herself. Not a thing that can only act when lifted into a chair, or stuck up on a platform; but a creature that will guide herself, answer questions, talk and eat like a rational being, in fact, perform the part of a society lady as well as any duchess of them all.'

'Moore,' I said, 'you must be mad.'

'Mad or not, I mean to try it. See here. Here is another automaton, that can walk, eat, turn its head, shut its eyes. That is common enough. Here is the brain power, the "anti-phonograph" that can speak and hear, indeed do anything but think. What is wanted but that the two should be combined?'

'My dear fellow,' I answered, 'it is easy to talk like that. I am a materialist, and would grant you more than most; but even in my view the brain is more than a mere machine. A man guides himself; *you* have to guide this automaton. How are you to get inside her and make her do all these things together at the proper time? Take a very simple example; your thing has to be sure to open its mouth when it speaks. How are you to ensure that the process which causes it to open its mouth, and the process which causes certain words to be uttered, shall take place simultaneously? Suppose the thing were to say, "I will sit down;" how are you to ensure that, at the proper moment, she shall go through the proper motions involved in sitting down? Remember, an error of half a second in your mysterious clockwork may make all the difference between your duchess occupying a dignified position in a chair and sprawling ingloriously on the floor. Why, think of the actions of but five minutes. She rises from a chair, she avoids the toes of the ladies and gentlemen in the room, she bows to a gentleman, she smiles – more or less hypocritically – at a lady, she makes a *bon-mot*, she laughs at somebody else's *bon-mots*; she even blows her nose. What countless simultaneous processes, not one of which must go wrong!'

Moore heard me through.

'Plausible enough,' he said, when I had finished; 'we shall soon see who is right. But tell me, should you not have said, a year ago, that the anti-phonograph was an impossibility?'

'Certainly I should.'

'Then a year hence you may alter your opinion on this point, as you have on that.'

'Hardly.'

'Who was it,' he asked, 'who lectured so vigorously on the folly of certain women of our time, and talked so largely about their utter inanity? Why, I remember your exact words. "The Society woman of our time," you proclaimed, "what is she but a doll? Her second-hand opinions, so daintily expressed, would not a parrot speak them as well? Her motions, her poses, which she thinks so statuesque, how affected, how mechanical they are! Is she a woman, this creature of the nineteenth century, or a puppet dressed up to go through a number of motions on the stage of London life, an automaton obeying the wire-pullings of the showman Fashion?" You meant all that for metaphor and eloquence, old fellow; and yet you object to my proving that it is all literal truth!'

'Prove it first,' I said.

'Only give me time,' he answered. 'But before you go,' he said, with a sudden impulse, as he saw me nearing the door, 'for God's sake not a word of this until I give you leave.'

'Make your mind easy,' I replied; 'a doctor knows how to keep a secret. When your lady goes out of order, send for a bottle of my emulsion, and I'll engage she'll trouble you no more!'

During the next few months I often thought of Moore and his hallucination; the picture of the poor fellow engaged on a hopelessly mad task often rose before my mind. I pitied him greatly. 'Another fine brain wasted,' I used to say. 'A man that more than rivalled Edison, spending the best years of his life over a mad chimera!' For I often visited him, and found him now despondent, now enthusiastic, but always dogged and impenetrably determined. I urged rest, a sea-voyage, anything to cure him of his brainsick folly. But he met me always with one reply: 'Rest *then;* not before.' Rest in the grave, poor fellow, I thought, as I noted his hectic cheek and staring bones. His fiery soul was fretting his body to decay.

At last, more than a year after our last conversation, amid the heap of letters lying on my table at breakfast, I came upon one that startled me. It was from Arthur Moore: short, but to the point.

'Success at last; come when you can.'

As soon as my round of visits was finished, I drove to his rooms. Mounting the stairs, I was ushered into the room by the most beautiful girl I had ever seen: a creature with fair hair, bright eyes, and a doll-like childishness of expression.

'Can he have married?' I thought, as I looked at her. 'How is Mr Moore?' I said aloud.

'Poorly to-day,' she replied. 'He will be here in a moment.'

Where and when had I heard that voice before? I seemed to know it, and yet I could not associate it with anybody. But I had no time to be perplexed; for in two or three seconds Moore appeared, looking ghastly and deathlike in his pallor.

'You are ill,' I said, when the first greeting was over. 'You have been overstraining yourself. You must really rest, or you will kill yourself.'

'Yes, I must,' he replied; 'and I think I shall. It has been toilsome work. But I think it was worth it, don't you?'

'How should I know?' I answered, 'I haven't seen it yet.'

'Yes, you have,' he said, smiling in spite of the pain that he must have been feeling.

I looked around, bewildered. I could see nothing but the same old room, and the strange girl sitting in an easy chair in the corner.

'You are mysterious,' I said, wondering not only at his words, but at the fact of his not having introduced me to the girl. 'Perhaps she is a nurse,' I thought; though no nurse in all my experience had ever looked like that.

'Wait a moment,' said Moore. Then, turning to the girl, he spoke a little louder.

'Mr Gladstone must be getting old now,' he said.

Again those clear, distinct, delicate tones, as the answer came,

'Eighty last birthday.'

I saw it all now. That beautiful, lady-like girl, that had ushered me into the room, whom I had taken for his wife, was an automaton! That doll-like expression was due to the fact that she *was* a doll. I was utterly astounded, and felt as if I were dreaming. The impossible had taken place. Moore sat by, enjoying my bewilderment; for a moment his weakness left him.

'Watch,' he said.

'Come here,' he said to the automaton.

The lady arose, after one second of apparent indecision, and approached him.

'Let me introduce to you Dr Phillips,' he said.

The lady smiled approval. (To this day I have never understood how Moore had managed to produce that smile – that fatal, monotonous, fascinating smile.)

'Dr Phillips, Miss Amelia Brooke.'

The lady bowed, and extended her hand.

'I am most happy to meet one of whom I have so often heard,' she said.

Could it be a reality? I felt more and more staggered. The lady stood perfectly still, her hands clasped before her. This fair creature not of flesh and blood? Impossible!

'You may go,' said Moore.

The thing moved back to her place, and sat down.

'What do you think of her?' he said aloud.

Before answering, I looked round to see where she was.

'Don't mind,' he said, laughing; 'she can't hear. I often have that feeling myself. You may discuss her as you please, and she won't be offended. She has one merit other women haven't, she is not touchy; but she has a failing the best of them have not, she can't blush. On the whole, however, I prefer her.'

'I am still almost incredulous,' I replied; 'indeed, until I have dissected her, and found pulleys instead of a liver, and eccentrics instead of a spleen, I shall hardly believe she isn't a woman in reality.'

'You can easily do so,' he said. 'Come here, Amelia.'

The creature rose, and came forward.

'Let Dr Phillips see your arm,' he said.

The lady showed me her arm, and turned up her sleeve. It did not need a moment's inspection to show me that this was not an arm of flesh and blood. What it actually was made of Moore would not tell me.

'Better than Madame Tussaud's, isn't it?' he said.

'Much better,' I replied. 'Might deceive anyone but a doctor.'

Passing my hand down to her wrist, I noted an exactly-moving pulse. So wonderfully was the human pulse imitated, that I believe anybody but one, like myself, trained to accurate discrimination, would have been deluded. I could not refrain from expressing my admiration.

'Yes,' said Moore, 'she will often have her arms bare, and there may be a good deal of hand-pressing and that sort of thing; so that I thought I ought to have everything right.'

'Does her heart beat too?' I asked.

'No,' he said; 'I wanted the space for other mechanism, so she has to do without a heart altogether. Besides,' he added, smiling, 'I wanted her to be a Society lady.'

'The thing will be worth thousands to you,' I said, when I had finished the examination of the creature's cutaneous covering. 'It is uncanny enough, and I can't say I like it, but it will draw. What a pity Barnum has gone! He would have given you a million dollars for it.'

Moore rose angrily.

'Do you think I will sell my own life-power for money?' he cried. 'That thing has cost me at least ten years of my life, and she shall never be exhibited like a two-headed nightingale, or a creature with its legs growing out of its pockets! She shall walk drawing-rooms like a lady, or I will break her to pieces myself!'

'My dear fellow,' I said, 'you are over-excited and ill. Surely you cannot know what you are saying?'

'I know well enough,' he answered doggedly. 'I have made a lady, you can't deny it; and a lady she shall be.'

'You have made a marionette,' I said, 'a very wonderful marionette, but nothing more. Never mind,' I went on, seeing him getting more passionate, 'all in good time. For the present you must rest and lie still.'

'Phillips,' he said, all the force of his character coming out in his face, 'I am determined that she shall be the beauty of the season. She shall eclipse them all, I tell you. What are they but dolls? And she is more than a doll, she is *Me*. I have breathed into her myself, and she all but lives; she understands and knows! Come, promise me you will not betray me!'

'Of course I will not,' I said; 'but you must give up this mad scheme. Consider, as an automaton she will make you for life; as a lady she will be found out in five minutes, and you will be laughed at. For your own sake pause!'

'Listen,' he said fiercely, all the veins in his forehead standing out like cords. I saw then how his own creation had possessed him till he was no longer master of himself.

'Listen,' he repeated. 'You call her an automaton. I tell you she is alive. See!'

He called the thing to him.

'Amelia,' he said, 'I have made you, and you are mine. Are you grateful?'

The creature smiled – the one smile she possessed, which she had, as I knew afterwards, for prince or peasant, man or maid.

'I can never forget what I owe you,' she replied.

'Kiss me then,' he said.

The thing bent down and kissed him obediently.

'You see,' he cried; 'is *that* an automaton?'

I felt sick and disgusted. I was already beginning to feel that hatred of this creature which afterwards filled me to overflowing.

'No,' I said, 'she is no automaton for *you*.'

'Then,' he replied, ignoring the implication of my words, 'will you introduce her to Society as a lady?'

'Never!' I answered. 'Moore, you are beside yourself.'

'Very well,' he rejoined; 'I will find somebody to do it instead. Remember, you have promised not to betray me, or to breathe a syllable of all this to anyone.'

Things had evidently gone far. As a doctor, I knew well how the constant brooding on a fixed idea often unhinges the strongest brain; but I confess that never in all my experience had I seen anything like this. It seemed to me like a possession of the devil. Would to God the accursed automaton were burnt to ashes, or had never been made! Again and again I wished I had never uttered the thoughtless words which had set all this in motion. But it was useless crying over the irremediable past. Something must be done, and done quickly, or poor Moore would make himself the laughing-stock of all London.

'Arthur,' I said, 'you must take a little time to rest before you do anything. Your physical nature is completely overwrought. Take my advice, and go to bed.'

'Will you help me?' he said obstinately.

'No,' I answered, losing patience at his confirmed stupidity.

'Then,' he said, 'I give –' What he would have added remains a secret, for at that moment his strength, tried too long, gave way, and he fell at my feet in a swoon.

Forgetting everything, save only that he was my friend, and that he was helpless, I applied the usual restoratives, and soon brought him round. I then rang the bell; a woman appeared.

'Your master is ill,' I said. 'Help me to put him to bed.'

The woman was a rough and rather dirty creature, without a trace of beauty in her, but she applied herself with alacrity to the task. We soon had poor Moore comfortably lying in bed; I gave the woman the proper directions, and left, promising to call again in the morning.

During all this time the automaton had remained motionless in the corner. I afterwards ascertained that Moore had concealed her more extraordinary powers from the other immates of the house, thinking they would be frightened; only letting them fancy she was a doll of the kind of Mr Maskelyne's Psycho. She had made no motion to assist her maker, 'grateful' as she was to him. I noted this with a sort of angry satisfaction.

'Moore,' I thought, 'said he preferred her to other women; on the whole I prefer the ugliest and dirtiest of them all to that beautiful but unfeeling creature.'

In a week care, and his own indomitable energy, restored Moore to something that did for health. He rose from his bed silent, impenetrable. He thanked me for my attention in polite terms; too polite, I thought, for the friend of so many years. Of his purpose, not a word. Had he forgotten it? Alas, no!

If there is any quality on which, more than on others, I fancy I have a right to plume myself, it is that of a firm will. What else, indeed, than an unflinching resolution could have brought me through the innumerable difficulties and struggles of my early life to the position I occupy at present? My enemies, indeed, have called me obstinate; but no one, not even a caricaturist, has ever represented me as flabby and pliable. Strong-willed I know I am; I have proved it over and over again – and yet there was one man before whom I was as wax, or as one of his own automata. That man was Arthur Moore. Years have gone by since he died; yet such is the spell his very memory casts over me that I feel even now that were he to come again and tempt me I should yield again, and yield almost willingly. Let those sneer who have never been tried as I was, who have never met the man of adamant, the King of Men, and who fancy themselves strong because they have always lived among the weak.

Shortly after his recovery, Moore called on me. There was a look of fixed resolve upon his face before which I quailed. It was the look of the monomaniac, that look which only comes after long brooding upon one idea.

'For the present she is perfect,' he said. 'I have taught her French – drawing-room French, I mean – and three songs. She can enter a room, bow, smile, and dance. If with these accomplishments she can't oust the other dolls and turn them green with jealousy for one season, I am much surprised. Now will you help me?'

'No,' I said. I was still struggling with the omnipotence of his will.

'You shall,' he replied. 'Others would do it if you refused; but it is my whim that you shall be the one to share my glory. Oh, what a time we shall have – how we shall laugh when we see it all, and think what fools men are!'

Again I tried to enter a feeble protest, but he overbore me. You ask how: I cannot tell. One thing I know, that if the thing were to happen again I should yield again. Call it magic, call it the force of personality; call it anything you like; but it overbore me. I yielded; I promised my assistance. We sat like two mischief-making children far into the small hours of the night, plotting how we could carry out the plan best, and arranging every detail so as to assure success and evade detection. Excuses and palliations coursed in undercurrents through my mind. I was a scientist, conducting a psychological experiment. I was a mere toy-maker, introducing into the world a rather elaborate toy. I was a Maskelyne, exposing the spiritualists. But on the whole I gave little heed to these thoughts. Moore had enslaved me, body and mind; I was carried away in a kind of drunken enthusiasm, and almost as feverishly excited as Moore himself. Nothing would now have stopped me. Would Frankenstein have paused the very hour before his creature took life? As for Moore, I believe he would have gone on with his designs in the very midst of the thunders of the Judgment Day itself.

Why should I linger over the early triumphs of our Phantasm? I was a fashionable doctor: I brought Miss Amelia Brooke out as a niece of mine. The Countess of Lorimer, one of my patients, undertook to pilot her through the first shoals of real life. Never shall I forget that first evening. Scarcely had she entered the room – it was at Lady Vandeleur's – when the eyes of all seemed, as if by magic, to be turned towards her. Exquisitely dressed, with a proud demeanour, with the step of a queen, she swept into the ball-room. She was my niece; I ought to have been proud of her; but I hated her with an intense loathing. Moore could do much with me, but he could not make me like this creature. Yet I was bound in nature to do all I could for her.

'Who is she?' said young Harry Burton to me. 'By Jove, she looks like a born queen.'

'You flatter me,' I replied. 'She is my niece. Good God,' I went on to myself, 'would that she were a born anything, instead of a made doll!'

'Oh,' rejoined Burton, 'lucky man that you are! Introduce me, will you?'

'With pleasure,' I answered.

I took him up and introduced him. During the ceremony I watched the creature carefully. No, there was no doubt about it. Such acting would deceive the Master of the Ceremonies in the court of Louis XIV himself. Every motion, every word, was exactly as it should be. How on earth had Moore managed it? I was almost deceived myself. Could this be after all a real creature of flesh and blood, substituted for the Phantasm? No; that detestable, beautiful smile was there – a smile which no woman ever wore, yet which none the less would be the bane of more than one man's existence.

Harry Burton danced many dances with her that night. When it closed, he was head over ears in love.

'Phillips,' he said in a brief interval, 'she is divine.'

'Devilish, rather,' I thought. 'Yes,' I said aloud, 'I think she is good-looking.'

'Good-looking!' he cried. 'What are all these painted dolls to her? *They* have nothing to say for themselves, *they* are mere bundles of conventionality; but *she* – she is all soul.'

'My boy,' I said warningly, 'you are evidently all heart. Be careful. Don't do anything rash. Dance with her, talk to her – do anything but fall in love with her.'

'Who talked of falling in love?' he said, astonished at my earnestness. 'I said nothing but that she was the finest girl in the room, and so she is, by Jove!'

'Nevertheless,' I said, 'it doesn't follow that she's worth falling in love with. Many a person *looks* all right, that's unsound within.'

'Why, here you are running down your own niece!'

'Not running her down; merely warning you. Besides,' I added smiling, 'she's only my niece by marriage.'

At this moment a new dance began, and Burton ran off to claim his partner. I remained, absorbed in not very pleasant reflections. Things were getting involved already. Moore had only told me he was making a woman; I had never calculated that he would make a coquette. What would come of it? I sat and watched her as she danced, dancing beautifully but a little mechanically, I thought, saying always the right things, answering questions always in the same way, and wearing at pretty regular intervals the same detestable smile. If I hated her before, I hated her tenfold now. I would speak to Moore, and put an end to it. A sudden cold – ordered to the South of France – and never let her come back. Good heavens, this creature never had a cold, never had a headache, never felt out of sorts: yet Moore said he had made a woman!

Slowly the evening dragged to its close – the most wearisome evening I had ever spent. The creature did not seem to tire; one dance or twenty was the same to her. The monotony of it all became at length intolerable to me. At the earliest decent opportunity I took my leave.

Moore had never been a Society man. Even to witness his own triumph he had refused to be drawn out of his retirement. Perhaps indeed he was afraid that his nerves might prove unequal to the strain of watching the creature that he had made rivalling the creatures that God – and the milliner – had made; perhaps he feared he might be tempted to betray all. At any rate, he stayed away; and it was with a feverish eagerness that he waited for the story of her successes from my lips.

'How did it all go off?' he said anxiously, as I made my promised call to tell him.

'As an experiment, very well,' I answered. 'There was no hitch, no failure. The success was only too monotonous. Human beings sometimes put their foot in it; she never. Would to God she might show now and then a little proneness to error!'

'You are queer,' Moore answered. 'Why should you grudge her her victories?'

'Arthur,' I said, 'the joke has gone quite far enough. Put a stop to it. Why go further? Think of the chances of detection – no, think of the far worse chances of success! Can't you see that the more skilful the deception the more dangerous will its consequences be? Already more than one young fellow has fallen head over ears in love with her. It is horrible to think of!'

'The fools!' he said, with a rather cynical smile. 'That is just the way with young fellows – never looking below the surface, looking only at the face. Why, Phillips, if they are taken in in that way they deserve to be taken in! *I* shall do nothing.'

He fixed his eyes upon me in conscious power. He knew that I could not resist him. Weakly, but inevitably, I gave way. I should do so again, with all the consequences as clearly before me as they are now.

So the thing went on, new developments constantly arising. I shall not stay to repeat them. The story is too painful to me; it is the story of my own insensate folly, and I do not care to dwell upon it. I hasten to the fatal ending.

Among the many deserters from the shrines of other goddesses, who thronged to pay their court to this new and strange divinity, two seemed to hold the divided first place in her favour. One was my young friend, Harry Burton; the other was handsome, impulsive, universally liked Dicky Calder. These two had been firm friends before, in spite of the fact that they had often flirted with the same girl. But it was impossible for two young fellows to love Amelia and continue to love each other. I watched the gradual change of their affection into distrust, jealousy, and hate; first with unutterable sorrow, and then with a sort of fatalistic shame. It was *my* fault, certainly; I could not hide that even from myself; but I seemed to be bound to go on in the path I had begun, committed to a course which knew no turning. Did I hesitate? A glance from Moore's commanding eyes impelled me onward. I repeat it, I am a strong-willed man; but Moore was the stronger.

To do Amelia justice, she was rigidly impartial between Burton and Calder. For both she had the same silvery tones, for both the same fascinating smile. To both, if they asked the same questions, she returned identically the same answers. To both she sang the same songs, with the crescendo in the same passages, and both, at the conclusion of the songs, received the same languishing, irresistible smile over the right shoulder, which made them her slaves on the spot.

At times the irony of the situation overcame me, and I could not restrain a laugh. 'Philosophers look forward to the time when men shall have automata as their slaves; but here are two young fools in willing, absurd slavery to an automaton, who bends them to her will as she pleases. Her *will!* I suppose she has no will, but she looks uncommonly like it. Let us call it caprice, then.' Then I would go off into a reverie. 'Are we all automata? Are we all mere chess-men on the board of life, moved hither and thither by a fate we cannot control?

Well, if we are, then Amelia is the queen, and Burton and Calder are two knights of opposing colours.'

One evening, a curious incident happened. Burton and Calder were as usual basking in the rays of their divinity, when by some mischance Amelia's brooch fell to the ground. Both the swains stooped to pick it up, but Burton was successful. Delighted at his triumph over his rival, he solicited the honour of re-fastening it. Calder watched him with jealous eyes. Suddenly a clumsy pair of waltzers, not looking where they were going, came hard into Burton. The brooch-pin was driven deep into the fair throat of Amelia. Burton started in horror; he began a savage oath, but stopping in time he pulled out the pin. Amelia had not uttered a sound.

Burton, speechless with dismay, was taking out his handkerchief to staunch the blood; Calder was holding the girl up as though she were fainting; a little crowd was gathering round them; when I, suddenly recollecting myself, rushed in. With the speed of lightning I whipped out my handkerchief and tied it round Amelia's neck.

'Stand back, all of you!' I said in a tone of command. Even Burton and Calder fell back a little.

My niece is very sensitive,' I said. 'The hurt is not great, but it would be as well that she should go home at once.' A terror had possessed me; an overmastering fear of detection held me as in a vice.

'I assure you, uncle, that I am not hurt at all,' said Amelia.

'Come along,' I said sternly.

I hurried her off, finding just time to bid my adieus to my hostess, and to console the dumbfounded Burton by saying there was no danger.

We drove, not home, but direct to Moore's lodgings. Hurriedly we went upstairs. Moore was still up. He seemed surprised to see us.

'What do you want?' he said.

'Fools that we are,' I answered. 'Why, we were within a hair's-breadth of detection. *The creature can't bleed.*'

'Why, what need has she to bleed?' he said.

'Every need,' I answered. 'Doesn't a girl bleed when a pin is driven a good inch into her throat?'

'What do you mean?'

I explained the circumstances, and how I hoped I had for this once staved off discovery. I had been just in time.

'No,' he said, when I had finished. 'I never thought she would need to bleed. Strange that I should have forgotten that! They say that murderers always forget just one thing, just one little thing! But *they* take pains to get rid of the blood, and I ought to take pains to have it there.'

'Give it up, Moore,' I said.

'Give it up! Never!' he shouted. 'Give it up for a few drops of blood! Rather would I drain my own veins into hers! Rather go out and kill somebody. What does Mephistopheles say? "Blood is a very peculiar sort of juice." But I will make it.'

Did I not know that no difficulties would deter him, that obstacles were in his eyes only incentives to further effort? If ever any man was ignorant of the word impossible, Moore was that man.

Miss Brooke was 'ill' for a few weeks from 'shock to the system.' At the end of that time I saw Moore again. He and the Phantasm were in the room together. He gave me a pin.

'Prick her,' he said.

I obeyed, not unwillingly; and to my horror something very like bleeding began.

'Yes,' said Moore, 'I have done it. I have looked up Shakespeare. Do you remember what Shylock says, to prove that a Jew is, after all, a man? "Hath not a Jew eyes? hath not a Jew hands, organs, dimensions, senses, affections, passions? fed with the same food, hurt with the same weapons, subject to the same diseases, healed by the same means, warmed and cooled by the same winter and summer, as a Christian is? If you prick us, do we not bleed? if you tickle us, do we not laugh? if you poison us, do we not die?" Now every one of these marks my Amelia has; so I say she is a genuine woman. Why, if you tickle her, she will laugh.'

'No one is likely to tickle her,' I said.

'No; but after our last experience it is well to be prepared for all emergencies.'

In this case, however, I did not make an experiment. Moore's word was enough. If the creature's smile was so detestable, what must her laugh be like?

After her time of seclusion, Amelia again appeared in Society, and was again the cynosure of all eyes, chiefly, however, of the four owned by Burton and Calder. These latter had never ceased to make inquiries after her health. I had often wondered whether Burton had noticed that the scratch of the pin had drawn no blood; but his conduct afterwards set me at ease. If he had seen it, he had probably thought that his Venus was too ethereal to bleed even the thinnest celestial ichor. The infatuation of youth can account for or put up with anything. At any rate, the young fellow admired her still; and Calder was equally possessed. In vain I assured them that she had no feeling; but this, though the literal truth, was met with derisive incredulity; and naturally I disliked to speak too often or too strongly against my niece. Blood, after all, even Amelia's manufactured blood, is thicker than water.

Though Amelia certainly could not feel, yet there was no doubt that in the future she would bleed if pricked, and I was free from anxiety on that score. But there was one thing which caused me considerable uneasiness. She was a girl of originality – indeed, I venture to think that there has never been a girl quite like her – yet there was a sameness, an artificiality about her which puzzled and alarmed me. To the same question she always and inevitably returned the same answer. On topics of the day she always had the same opinion, expressed in the same words. My rival, Sir John Bolus, who didn't like her for some reason or other, used to say that in her company he always felt as if talking to a very well-trained parrot. She uttered her opinions as if they had been learnt verbatim from someone else. Now there is nothing a true woman ought to do so frequently as to change her mind. Everybody should hear from her lips something different from what everybody else hears. It was on this point that I felt that Moore had failed; and it was from this that somehow or other I vaguely anticipated disaster. My apprehensions were but too well founded.

The time drew near for Calder and Burton to declare themselves. I need not say that, closely as I watched the doings of Amelia, I was not present on these auspicious occasions. But I can distinctly assert, nevertheless, from my knowledge of human nature, that the language of Calder, who came second, was almost precisely the same as that of Burton, who had the first chance. Hence it followed, with mathematical certainty, that Amelia's reply would be the same to both. Here was a pretty predicament! What I had blamed in her was her unwomanly constancy; but this very constancy had led – as I was sure both *a priori* and from the happy faces of the two young men – to a display of fickleness unparalleled in the whole history of womankind. Within an hour after accepting Burton the faithless creature accepted Calder in almost identically the same terms! Even the most heartless of coquettes had surely never been guilty of such conduct as this.

All this, however, was for the present merely a plausible conjecture, based upon a more or less certain knowledge of character. To make sure of it, I determined to ask. The result but too sadly confirmed my fears. Burton was almost delirious with joy.

'She is mine,' he said; 'and that beast Calder was never in it with her. To think that I should ever have been afraid of a cad like that!'

I congratulated him as in duty bound, and spent an hour with him which may have been pleasant to him, but became very tedious to me: so difficult was it to get him off his one eternal topic and induce him to talk like a rational being. At last, however, I managed to effect my escape, and made my way to Calder. He also received me very graciously.

'Old man,' he said, 'I have good news to tell you. Amelia has just consented to be engaged to me.'

'Indeed!' I replied; 'I am very pleased to hear it. You are a happy man, Dick.'

'Yes,' he said, 'happier than I deserve. But what delights me almost as much as having won her is that she never gave a thought to that fellow Burton. If I had had any sense I must have seen that a girl like her could never be taken in by a wretched fellow like him; but somehow I managed to be jealous of him. Well, *that's* all over, thank goodness. I really believe I shall get to like him now I'm sure he can do me no harm.'

And so the young fellow chattered on, cutting me to the heart with almost every sentence that he uttered. What a dreadful awakening I was preparing for him! For of course the awful truth must be told him, that he and his rival had fallen in love with a sham. It would be an awkward moment for both of us. Should I tell him now, and get it over? On the whole I preferred to put it off, and consult Moore first. His fertile brain would suggest a way out of the difficulty. Perhaps he would make a second automaton that would do for one of the rival suitors, while the other kept to Amelia. At any rate, I preferred to get his advice before acting. He had made the Phantasm bleed; might he not get us out of this still more unpleasant position?

I told him of the new complication. To my surprise he made light of it.

'Well?' he said when I had finished my recital.

'Well?' I replied, 'I should think that was enough.'

'Why,' he said, 'I can see nothing wonderful in that. The wonder would be if they *hadn't* proposed to her. Women have had offers before now.'

'But you can't intend to let things go on as they are?' I cried.

'That's exactly what I *do* intend,' he answered. 'Why should I interfere?'

'But think of it for one moment,' I said. 'Two men in love with the same automaton: two men in the position of accepted lovers at the same moment! Think of even *one* man in that position! How awful it is – why, it is too dreadful to think of!'

'Then I shan't think of it,' he answered coolly. 'My dear fellow, what is there so strange in it all? Men have been in love with stone-like women before this. Men have given themselves up to heartless and soulless abstractions before this. Anyone who gets my Amelia will get *something*, at any rate, not a mere doll.'

The plain fact dawned on me that Moore's extraordinary success had turned his brain. He had put so much of himself into his automaton that he had positively begun to regard her as a real living being, in whose veins flowed his own blood, in whose nostrils was his own breath. Eve was not more truly bone of Adam's bone than this Amelia was part and parcel of Moore's life. There was a mysterious union between them which gave me an uncanny feeling of sorcery. Could it be that by some unholy means Moore had succeeded in conveying some portion of his own life to this creature of his brain? I tried to dismiss the thought, for I am a man of science; yet it recurred again and again.

Moore was monomaniac on this point; yet, strange to say, my conviction of his lunacy did not lessen the influence he had acquired over me. His intellect was as keen, his will as powerful, as ever; and in spite of the utter monstrosity of his plans, and their inhuman cruelty, I lent myself to their fulfilment, and went desperately on to the bitter end. Let me hasten to the final catastrophe.

Burton and Calder were engaged to Amelia. It may be easily understood that now and then they came into collision. Sometimes things looked strange to them. Calder once demanded an explanation of his *fiancée* as to the frequency of Burton's visits. She gave him an account that satisfied him, and sealed it with a smile and a kiss that made him feel like a villain for ever doubting her. People wondered at the confidence with which both the young men asserted that they were the favoured suitor, and admired the daring skill with which Amelia played off one against the other. No one warned the young men; it was none of our business to interfere with them. English people do not care for meddling. As for me, had I not done enough by giving both of them a very plain piece of advice at the very outset, to which neither of them had paid the slightest attention, beyond insinuating that I was jealous of my own niece?

In such matters one young man is remarkably similar to another. Their very modes of speech tend to become the same. In asking Amelia to fix the day, need it be wondered at that they used precisely the same terms as have been used by all young men from the day when that nameless suitor of 'pretty Jane' promised to buy the ring for his beloved? The result may be easily foreseen. Amelia, by some hidden law of her being, for which not she but perhaps Moore was to blame, could not help fixing the same day for both. Had a third candidate appeared on the scene, she would have fixed the same day for him also.

When I had heard this last fatal *dénoûment*, I confess that even Moore's influence could not keep me from taking a step on my own account. I would not destroy Amelia, much as I hated her for the trouble she had caused me. Something seemed to tell me that her death would be the certain death of Moore, whose life was bound up in hers as closely as the life of Jacob was bound up in that of Benjamin. By some subtle process, every time danger threatened Amelia, Moore's spirits seemed to sink; every time she surmounted the danger his spirits rose again. He had put himself into her. I would not destroy her; but I went to Calder and I gave him a pretty plain hint as to the position of affairs between her and Burton. He would not believe me.

'If I thought she was false,' he said, 'I would stab her where she stood, were it at the very altar. But it cannot be. She has pledged herself to me, and mine she is!'

'I know it for a fact,' I answered, 'that she has promised to marry Burton on the 29th of February.'

'The twenty-ninth!' he cried. 'Why, that is *my* day, the day on which she has promised to marry me!'

'Precisely so,' I said. 'What she means to do I don't know.'

'But I know what *I* mean to do,' he answered gloomily. 'I will have it out with her.'

'No violence!'

'None at all. Don't fear me. By God, what a heartless creature! But it can't be true. You are deceiving me!'

'Too true. But find out for yourself.'

'I took my leave, and went home. I did not intend to see Moore; I knew the strange spell of his eyes, and that even now I might be unable to resist his will.

I afterwards ascertained what Calder's plan was. He made no inquiry from Amelia; he simply went and begged her to put off the day of his marriage a month, from the twenty-ninth of February to the last of March. She readily agreed. He then went off to a shop he knew, and bought a sharp Spanish dagger.

The day of the marriage drew near, and nearer. Every preparation was completed. It was to be fashionable. St George's was got ready in expectation of a large assemblage of people. At length the eventful morning dawned. I was to give the bride way to Burton, as after the postponement of Calder's wedding he was the only bridegroom left in the race. We came out and stood before the altar. As I passed along I noticed two figures in different parts of the building, both familiar to me. They were Moore and Calder. The former was untidy, evidently excited and restless. The latter was scrupulously neat; but he had a strangely determined look on his face. One hand was hidden under the breast of his frock-coat.

The service proceeded. Fancy a girl like this being told she was a daughter of Abraham, so long as she was not afraid with any amazement! Certainly a cooler, less perturbed daughter of the patriarch I never saw. She gave the responses in a clear, musical voice. They came to the fatal question – 'Wilt thou have this man to be thy husband?' Before she could answer 'I will,' there was a sudden confusion; a man rushed forward, drew forth a dagger from his breast, and shouting 'You shall not!' stabbed Amelia to the heart – or rather through the left side of her bodice. She fell to the ground, striking her head heavily as she fell against the rail. There was a whirr, a rush. The anti-phonograph was broken. I bent over her, and opened her dress to staunch the wound. Moore had made no provision for her bleeding *there*. As I drew out the dagger, it was followed by a rush of sawdust.

In the confusion of the strange discovery, no one noticed that a real death was taking place not twenty feet away. As the sexton was clearing out the church, be noticed a man asleep in one of the pews, leaning against a pillar. He went up and touched him; but there was no answer. He shook him; but the man was as heedless as Baal. It was Arthur Moore, and he was dead. He had put his life into his masterpiece; his wonderful toy was broken, and the cord of Moore's life was broken with it.

And as for me, why, I am no longer a fashionable physician. As I write, there are men about me, who talk of me as a *patient*.